DON'T WAKE DAD!

Obi

Nadia

Written by
EDEN WELLS

Illustrated by
SHARON DAVEY

In the middle of a forest,
in a cosy little lair,

This Ladybird book belongs to

....

For my son Max – aka The Sleep Thief
E.W.

To Neve and Alex, always
S.D.

LADYBIRD BOOKS

UK | USA | Canada | Ireland | Australia
India | New Zealand | South Africa

Ladybird Books is part of the Penguin Random House group of companies
whose addresses can be found at global.penguinrandomhouse.com.

www.penguin.co.uk   www.puffin.co.uk   www.ladybird.co.uk

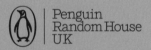

Penguin
Random House
UK

First published 2022
001

Written by Eden Wells
Illustrated by Sharon Davey
Copyright © Ladybird Books Ltd, 2022

Printed in Italy

The authorized representative in the EEA is Penguin Random House Ireland,
Morrison Chambers, 32 Nassau Street, Dublin D02 YH68

A CIP catalogue record for this book is available from the British Library

ISBN: 978–0–241–56059–4
All correspondence to:
Ladybird Books Ltd
Penguin Random House Children's
One Embassy Gardens, 8 Viaduct Gardens
London SW11 7BW

two bear cubs wake up with a start
– there's a party to prepare!

Shhh!
Don't wake Dad!

But this shindig is a secret
    – a surprise for Papa Bear.

He's fast asleep, he's snoring,
    and if he wakes, well then . . . BEWARE!

The twins must be so silent,
there's still so much to do:

balloons
to blow,

and cakes
to bake,

and chocolate
to fondue.

And then a knock strikes at the door,
a **BANG** that shakes the ground!

But who would call at such a time?
How dare they make a sound!

Dear me, it's only Uncle Doug.
He gave the twins a fright.

The wolves turn up, and then the mice –
the skunks must wait outside.

Marcel just won't fit through the door –
his antlers are too wide!

BANG!

THUMP!

THUD!

"Don't wake Dad!" the twins remark.
"We need you to be quiet!
The party is not ready yet,
so please don't start a riot!"

"The porcupines are near balloons!
Please move them all away!

The deer and mice are arguing . . .

At last, they call a truce.

Against all odds, Dad's not awake.
Then one balloon slips loose . . .

The bear cubs both
chase after it . . .

A gust blows
it astray.

It flutters upward,
out of reach,

and shoots off the
wrong way!

It blows straight through the window,
and enters Dad's dark room!

It hovers over his sharp teeth

and breaks the silence . . .

BOOM!

A roar erupts from in the lair –
Papa Bear is on the prowl.
His footsteps crash, he beats his chest
and shrieks the deepest growl.

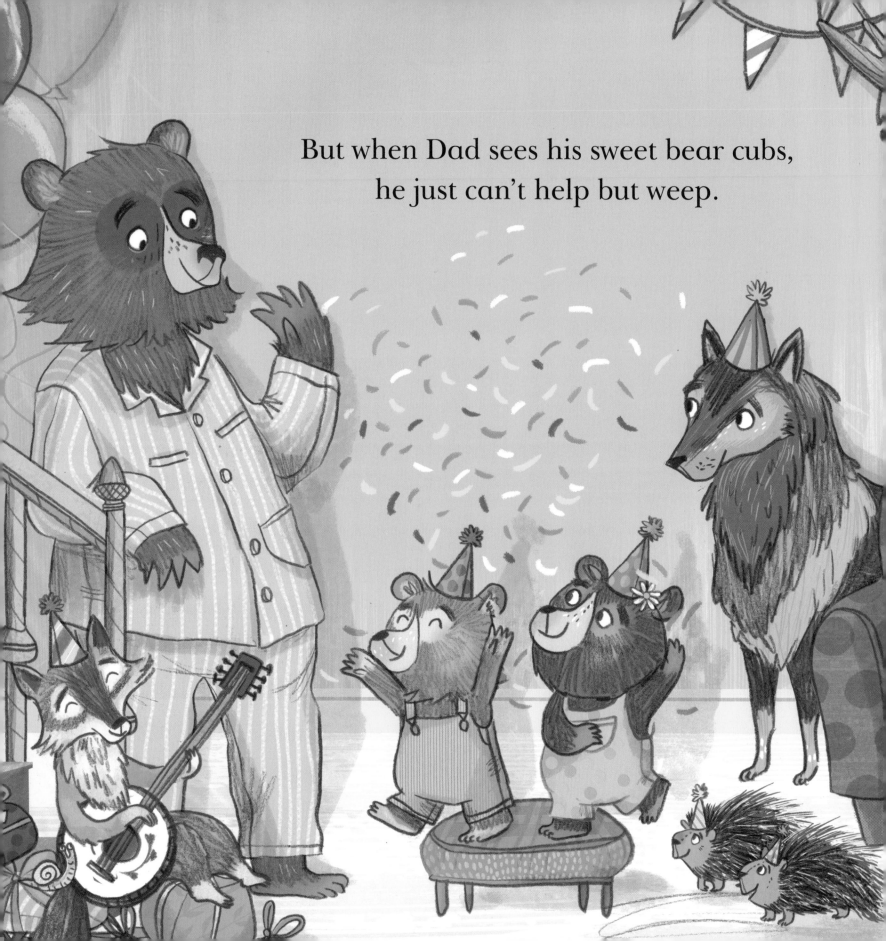

But when Dad sees his sweet bear cubs,
he just can't help but weep.

"We wanted to say thank you, Dad,
for everything you've done.
For the school runs and the stories,
the dad jokes and the fun.

You cheer us up when we are sad
and catch us when we fall.
And now you're up and wide awake . . .
so HUGGY BEARS FOR ALL!"